GREENWILLOW BOOKS, NEW YORK

COLORS EVERYWHERE

TANA HOBAN

Printed in Singapore by Tien Wah Press   First Edition   10   9   8   7   6   5

Library of Congress Cataloging-in-Publication Data
Hoban, Tana.
Colors everywhere   by Tana Hoban.
p.   cm.
ISBN 0-688-12762-2 (trade).
ISBN 0-688-12763-0 (lib. bdg.)
1. Color—Pictorial works—Juvenile literature.
[1. Color—Pictorial works.]   I. Title.
QC495.5.H6   1994   535.6—dc20
93-24847   CIP   AC

For Holly, John, Christopher, Kirk and Oliver—who color my life—

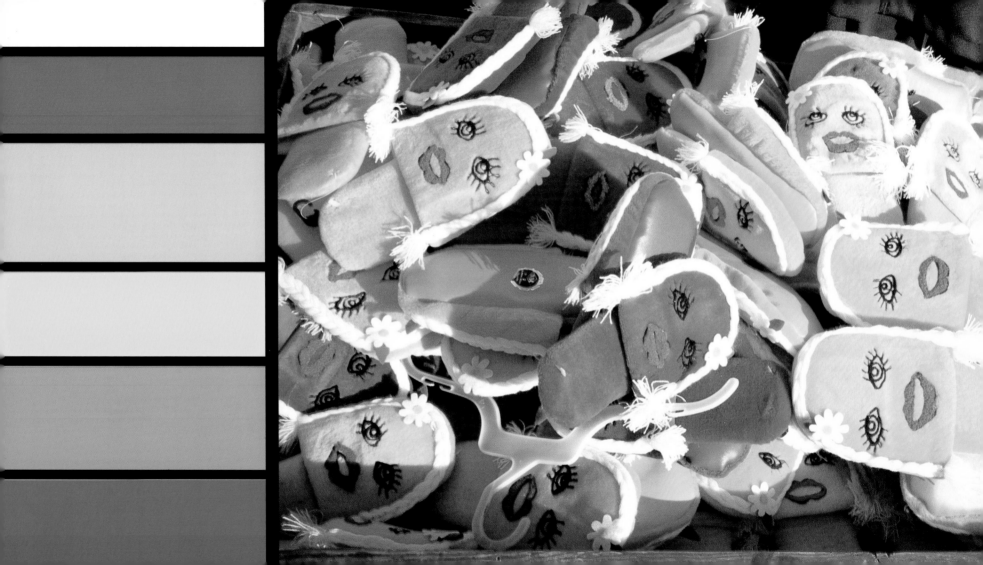

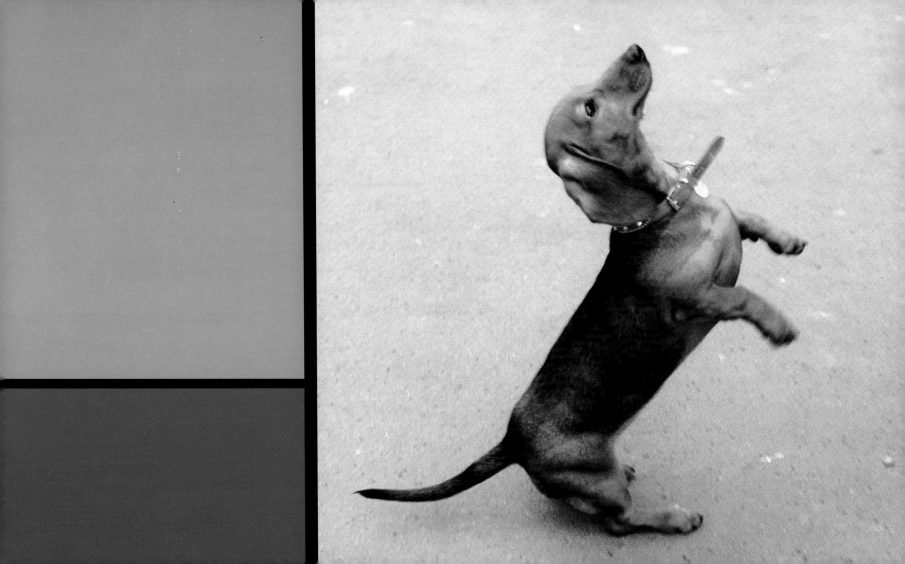

TANA HOBAN's photographs have been exhibited

at the Museum of Modern Art in New York City and in galleries

around the world. Her more than forty books for children are

internationally known and loved, and include such classics

as *Count and See*, *Take Another Look*, *All About Where*, and

the seminal board books *Black on White* and *White on Black*.

Born in Philadelphia, she now lives in Paris with her husband.